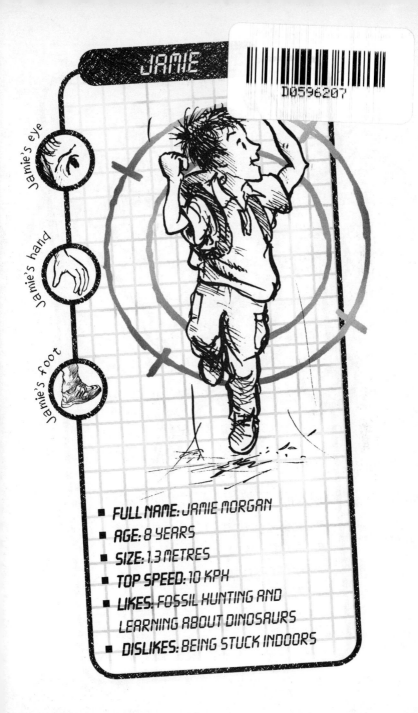

JAMIE

D0596207

Jamie's eye

Jamie's hand

Jamie's foot

- **FULL NAME:** JAMIE MORGAN
- **AGE:** 8 YEARS
- **SIZE:** 1.3 METRES
- **TOP SPEED:** 10 KPH
- **LIKES:** FOSSIL HUNTING AND
  LEARNING ABOUT DINOSAURS
- **DISLIKES:** BEING STUCK INDOORS

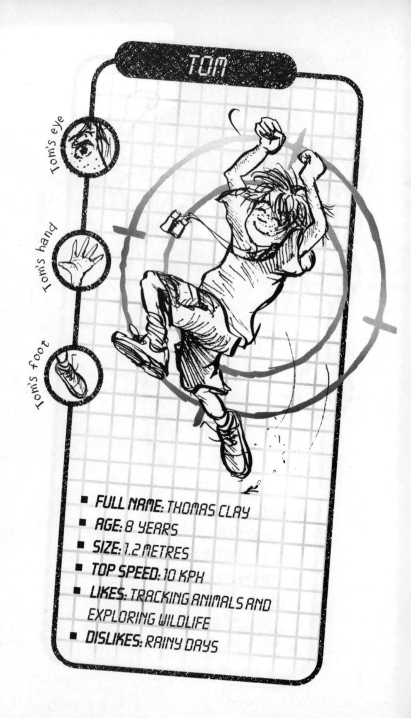

TOM

Tom's eye

Tom's hand

Tom's foot

- **FULL NAME:** THOMAS CLAY
- **AGE:** 8 YEARS
- **SIZE:** 1.2 METRES
- **TOP SPEED:** 10 KPH
- **LIKES:** TRACKING ANIMALS AND EXPLORING WILDLIFE
- **DISLIKES:** RAINY DAYS

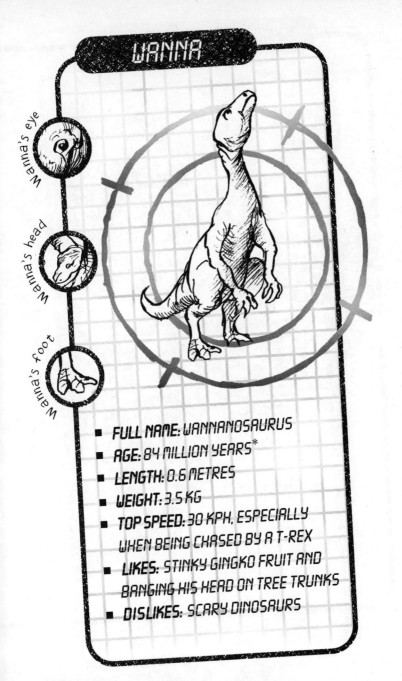

WANNA

Wanna's eye

Wanna's head

Wanna's foot

- **FULL NAME:** WANNANOSAURUS
- **AGE:** 84 MILLION YEARS*
- **LENGTH:** 0.6 METRES
- **WEIGHT:** 3.5 KG
- **TOP SPEED:** 30 KPH, ESPECIALLY WHEN BEING CHASED BY A T-REX
- **LIKES:** STINKY GINGKO FRUIT AND BANGING HIS HEAD ON TREE TRUNKS
- **DISLIKES:** SCARY DINOSAURS

*NOTE: SCIENTISTS CALL THIS PERIOD THE LATE CRETACEOUS

DINOSAUR COVE

8

Landslips where clay and fossils are

Muddy beach

High Tide beach line

DINO CAVE

Low tide beach line

Sea

Smuggler's Point

9

A Jurassic Adventure

Dinosaur Cove™

Rescuing the
Plated Lizard

Special thanks to Jane Clarke

To Susan – a great mother, loving sister and
best friend – R.S.

To Christopher – M.S.

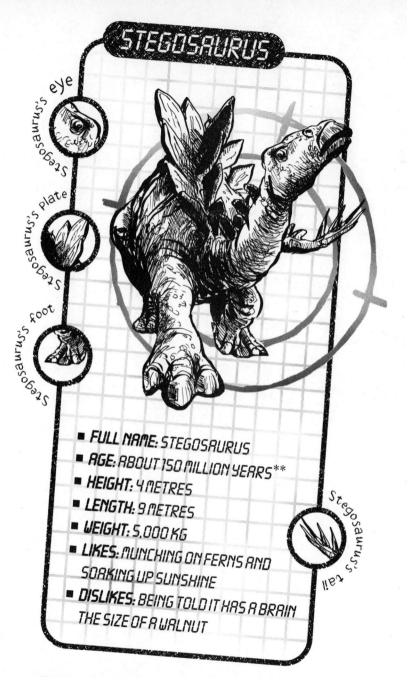

STEGOSAURUS

Stegosaurus's eye

Stegosaurus's plate

Stegosaurus's foot

Stegosaurus's tail

- **FULL NAME:** STEGOSAURUS
- **AGE:** ABOUT 150 MILLION YEARS**
- **HEIGHT:** 4 METRES
- **LENGTH:** 9 METRES
- **WEIGHT:** 5,000 KG
- **LIKES:** MUNCHING ON FERNS AND SOAKING UP SUNSHINE
- **DISLIKES:** BEING TOLD IT HAS A BRAIN THE SIZE OF A WALNUT

NOTE: SCIENTISTS CALL THIS PERIOD THE JURASSIC

'Dino World here we come!'

Jamie Morgan and his best
friend, Tom Clay, clattered down
the stairs of the old lighthouse
ready for a new adventure. They

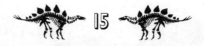

burst into the museum on the
ground floor and skidded to a halt
in front of Jamie's dad.

'It's good to hear you being so
enthusiastic about the museum,'
Jamie's dad said. He was kneeling on
the floor beside a sandpit, arranging
plastic trowels around the edge.

Jamie spluttered. 'Er um . . . it's awesome!' He hadn't been talking about his dad's fantastic dinosaur museum. He'd meant the secret world of real dinosaurs that he and Tom had discovered in a hidden cave.

'Visitors will love your new exhibit,' Tom said to change the subject. He took a trowel and poked at a cookie-sized fossil half-buried in the sand. 'That's an ammonite.'

'If you dig it out and match it with the ammonites on display you can find out what time period it comes from,' Mr Morgan told him.

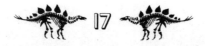

Permian

Triassic

Jurassic

Cretaceous

Jamie looked into the glass display case against the wall. Each ammonite fossil was carefully labelled with time periods, including Permian, Triassic, Jurassic, and Cretaceous.

Jamie started rummaging in his backpack. 'Can you tell when my ammonite is from?' he asked, pulling out the one he'd found on his first day on the beach in Dinosaur Cove.

Jamie's dad studied the fossil closely and checked it against the ones in the display case. 'It has deep ridges and the ribs are complete circles around the outer edge. That means it's definitely Late Cretaceous.'

Jamie smiled at Tom. Their secret cave led to a world with real, live Late Cretaceous dinosaurs like triceratops and velociraptors.

'Ammonites are like keys to the past,' Jamie's dad went on. 'Scientists use them to help date the rock layers where they're found.'

'Cool,' Tom said.

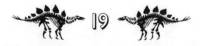

'We're going
exploring,' Jamie
said. 'You can
keep my ammonite
for the exhibit.'

'Thanks, son.' Jamie's dad
buried it under the sand with the
other ammonites. 'Have fun!'

'We will.'

Jamie and Tom dashed out of the
lighthouse and ran as fast as they
could along the beach and up the

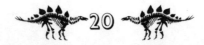

cliff to the old smugglers' cave.

'I can't wait to see Wanna again,' Tom said as they wriggled through the gap at the back of the cave into the secret chamber. They'd met the wannanosaurus on their first trip to Dino World and the little dinosaur had been their friend ever since. It was actually their dinosaur friend's fossilized footprints that had transported them into Dino World.

'Any second now . . .' Jamie could feel the excitement bubbling up inside him as he put his feet into Wanna's fossilized footprints. What dinosaurs would they meet today?

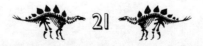

'One, two, three . . .' Jamie headed towards the rock face. 'Four, five—OUCH!' Instead of emerging into Dino World, Jamie smacked into the solid rock.

Tom bumped into the back of him. 'What happened?'

Jamie rubbed his scraped knee. 'I don't know.' He shone his torch on the fossil footprints.

'You must be doing it wrong,' Tom said. 'Let me go first.' He took five confident steps and then his head whacked against the cave wall. 'OW!' he

yelled, rubbing his forehead. 'It's
not working!'

Jamie fought down a wave of panic. 'We must be doing something different.'

'We're walking like we always do and wearing what we always wear,' Tom said. 'What's in your backpack?'

Jamie tipped out the contents and shone his torch on them. 'Fossil Finder, compass, map, binoculars, sandwiches.' He stuffed everything back in.

'Even the sandwiches are the same—cheese and your grandad's pickle.' Tom sighed.

'But something must have

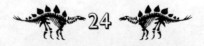

changed,'
Jamie insisted.

'Maybe something's missing,'
Tom said.

'My ammonite!' Jamie jumped to
his feet. 'It's been with us every time
we've been to Dino World. We've got
to get it back!'

They raced to the old lighthouse
and the main door was still shut. The
museum hadn't yet opened for the day.

'We're in luck,' Tom said as Jamie pulled open the heavy door. They tiptoed into the museum and peered cautiously around.

'There's no sign of Dad. Quick!' Jamie and Tom each grabbed a trowel and dug in the sand. Soon, they each had a big pile of ammonites to look through.

'That's the lot.' Jamie put down his trowel and started looking through

the fossils. 'My ammonite is black with shiny gold ridges, and it's about as big as a yo-yo.'

'We should put the wrong ones back,' Tom suggested.

'Good idea,' Jamie agreed. They reburied the fossils that were too big or too small or made of the wrong type of stone until only two were left.

'Which one is it?' Tom asked, looking at the two similar fossils.

'It's hard to tell,' Jamie said, 'but I think it's this one.'

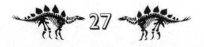

Tom agreed and Jamie stuffed the ammonite he was holding into his pocket whilst Tom pushed the other one back into the sandpit. They slipped out of the door and ran back to the cave as fast as they could.

'Fingers crossed.' Jamie fitted his feet into Wanna's fossilized footprints. 'One, two, three . . .' He walked slowly towards the wall, bracing himself for impact with the solid rock. 'Four . . .' Jamie held his hands out in front of him as he stepped forward. 'Five!'

He felt a sudden rush of hot, humid air and his ears rang with

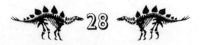

the calls of strange jungle creatures.
He took a deep breath and his
nostrils filled with the
peaty smell of warm
leaf-mould. Jamie
opened his eyes.
Tom was standing
next to him. They
were back in Dino
World.

'Hurrah!' Tom
shouted.

Jamie looked
behind him to
check that their
usual way home

was there and was relieved to see
the muddy version of the fossilized
footprints leading away from the back
of the cave.

'Everything is back to normal,'
Jamie declared. 'Let's go!' Jamie and
Tom dashed out of the cave and set
off through the gingko trees.

Jamie parted the creepers and
stopped dead. 'What happened to
the view?'

Tom's mouth dropped open. 'I have
no idea.'

The hillside view over the grassy
plains, the winding river, Fang
Rock, and Far Away Mountains had

disappeared. Instead, all they could
see was the trunks of more jungle
trees. Dino World had changed!

CHAPTER 2

'Where are we?' Tom asked.

'There's only one way to find out.'
Jamie looked up for the tallest gingko
tree, grabbed a low branch and
swung himself up. Tom climbed on
behind him. They hauled themselves

up through the
sturdy branches until
they could see out
over Dino World.

Tom wrapped his legs around
a branch and looked through his
binoculars. 'The lagoon is gone!'
He gulped. 'And there are hills in

the south-east where the marsh should be.'

'And the White Ocean's a lot nearer,' Jamie added, gazing across the sea towards the horizon. A dark shape broke the surface of the bright blue water.

'Pass me the binoculars.' Jamie hung on to the tree trunk and focused on where the creature had appeared. A crocodilian head on the end of a snake-like neck came into view, followed by an elephant-sized grey-green body. The creature lay basking on the surface, lazily moving its four huge flippers.

'Cool!' Jamie declared. 'I'm glad we didn't catch anything like that when we went crabbing.' Jamie handed the binoculars back to Tom.

'We'd never have got it in the crab bucket.' Tom chuckled. He twisted round with the binoculars still to his eyes.

'The Plains are still there, but the Far Away Mountains aren't just mountains any more,' he said. 'They look like volcanoes.'

Tom handed the binoculars to Jamie and pushed his curly red hair behind his sticky-out ears. 'What's going on?' he asked.

Jamie slowly scanned the horizon.
At the edge of the plains, a pair
of long-necked dinosaurs were
grazing on the top branches of tall
conifer trees.

'Brachiosaurs,' Jamie whispered.
'I thought they were from the
Jurassic. I can't see *any* of the
Cretaceous dinosaurs we usually see.

No triceratops,
no ankylosaurs,
no t-rex . . .'
     Tom laughed. 'I'm
glad about the last one!'
     At the sound of Tom's laughter
a pair of crow-sized creatures
perching in the tree above them
began squawking and flapping their
electric blue feathers.

'They've got claws at the end of their wings,' Jamie said in surprise.

'And beaks full of tiny teeth,' Tom added. 'What are they?'

'I'll find out.' Jamie wedged himself between the trunk and the branch he was sitting on and took out his Fossil Finder. He typed *BIRD WITH TEETH AND CLAWS* into the search box.

'ARCHAEOPTERYX,' Jamie read.
'PART BIRD AND PART DINOSAUR, DATING FROM THE JURASSIC PERIOD ABOUT A HUNDRED AND FIFTY MILLION YEARS AGO.'
He snapped the Fossil Finder shut and shoved it into his backpack. 'You know what this means?'

Jamie and Tom looked at each other. 'We're in the Jurassic!' they yelled, holding on to the tree trunk with one hand and giving each other a high five with the other.

Jamie's heart leapt for joy. They'd arrived in a different time. They had a whole new Dino World to explore and a whole new set of dinosaurs to see!

CHAPTER 3

Jamie and Tom scrambled eagerly
down the gingko tree and plunged
into the steamy Jurassic jungle. A
cloud of insects the size of paper
aeroplanes, with long dangly legs,
whirred into the air around them.

'Do Jurassic bugs have stings?' Jamie asked nervously, flapping his hands as he tried to keep them from settling on his head.

'I hope not!' Tom muttered. 'We need a Jurassic bug swat.' He wiped the sweat from his hands on his T-shirt, then tried to snap off one of the stems of the horsetail ferns

that towered above
their heads. He bent
and twisted it but the
thick, jointed rod-like stem
refused to break.

'These ferns are really
tough,' he muttered.

'Here.' Jamie tore off a
couple of smaller fronds and
handed one to Tom. They
swished at the insects as
they pushed on through
the jungle.

'So, how did we come out of the cave into a different time?' Tom wondered aloud.

Jamie pulled the new ammonite fossil out of his pocket. 'The ammonite I gave to Dad was from the Late Cretaceous. I reckon this must be a different ammonite from the Jurassic.'

'I get it,' Tom said. 'Changing the ammonite has changed the time period. It's like your dad said: ammonites really are the key to the past.' He looked sad suddenly. 'But what about Wanna? Will we ever see him again?'

'He'll be waiting for us in the Cretaceous,' Jamie reasoned, stuffing the fossil back in his pocket. 'When we get back to the lighthouse, we'll find the other ammonite. We can still visit him.'

'It won't be the same exploring without Wanna,' Tom said. 'But I guess we have a whole new world to discover. Did you know that the biggest plant eaters that ever lived were in the Jurassic?'

'Yeah, I did.' Jamie grinned, and then looked serious. 'But if there were loads of plant eaters in the Jurassic, wouldn't there have been loads of meat eaters eating them?'

Tom nodded. 'Allosaurs were nearly as big as t-rex, and just as fierce. And ornitholestes were the size of wolves and hunted in packs. They'd stalk their prey, then creep up and their sharp teeth would—'

Suddenly, the ferns in front of them began to rustle.

'Meat eaters! Hide!' Jamie yelled, hurling himself into a big pile of dead ferns.

Tom burrowed in beside him. Jamie poked his finger through the steamy leaf mould and made a peep-hole.

'What's coming?' Tom whispered.

'The ground didn't shake,' Jamie said, 'so it can't be an allosaurus.'

'Maybe a pack of ornitholestes is stalking us.' Tom shuddered.

Jamie held his breath as the ferns rustled fiercely. What scary dinosaur would they come face-to-face with?

CHAPTER 4

A small bony reptilian head poked
out of the ferns.

'Wanna?' Jamie gasped in
amazement as the little Cretaceous
dinosaur bounded out of the Jurassic
ferns. Wanna stood on his back legs,

Grunk!
Grunk!
Grunk!

tilted his head to one side, and gazed
down at him with twinkling eyes.

Grunk? It sounded almost like
a question.

'It is; it's Wanna!' Tom poked his head out, pulling pieces of rotting fern out of the neck of his T-shirt.

Grunk! Grunk! Grunk!

Wanna bobbed his head up and down, grunking ecstatically as Jamie and Tom leapt out of the mound of dead ferns and shook themselves off.

'How did you get here, Wanna?' Jamie asked. 'You don't belong in the Jurassic.'

'He must be tied to the magic, somehow,' Tom guessed. 'After all, it is Wanna's fossil footprints that brought us to Dino World.'

'The Jurassic is even better now
that Wanna's in it,' Jamie agreed.
'Do you think he's been here before?'
'It doesn't look like it,'
Tom replied.
Wanna was biting
chunks out of the horsetail
ferns and spitting them
out in disgust. He stopped
and looked hopefully at
Jamie's backpack.
'Oh, dear,' Jamie said.
'He's hungry and we didn't

pick him any of those stinky gingko fruits he likes so much.'

'Never mind that,' Tom whispered, pointing into the sea of tall ferns not far from them. 'I can see a dinosaur.' The tip of a reddish-brown back plate was moving through the greenery. 'It looks like a shark's fin,' he said.

'There weren't any land-sharks in the Jurassic.' Jamie punched Tom on the arm.

Jamie kept his eye on the rustling ferns and caught a glimpse of a small reptilian head the size of Wanna's, with a beaky nose, snuffling through the ferns. There were more of the plate-like fins on the shoulders.

'That could be a stegosaurus!' Tom declared, as the dinosaur moved out of sight among the greenery.

'It could be,' Jamie replied. 'But there was another plated dinosaur: the kentrosaurus. It had spikes on its back as well as the plates near its neck. We have to get a clearer look to be sure.'

They hurried through the ferns, closer to where they spotted the dinosaur.

'It could even be a new sort of dinosaur,' Tom whispered as they crept along. 'People who discover a new dinosaur get to name them. I'd call it tomosaurus.'

'That's not a scientific name,' Jamie retorted. 'Platey-o-saurus would be better.'

Tom thought for a minute. 'How about we call it tomjamosaurus?'

'It's a deal.' Jamie grinned. 'Though jatomosaurus sounds good, too.'

Jamie, Tom, and Wanna tracked the dinosaur's trail through the ferns and into a clump of spindly conifer trees.

57

Suddenly, Wanna gave a grunk and rushed past Jamie, licking his lips. 'Hey, watch where you're going, Wanna!' Jamie called.

Jamie and Tom hurried after their dinosaur friend. Wanna burst out of the ferns into the sunlight.

Suddenly, on the hillside clearing in front of them, there were fifteen reddish-brown speckled dinosaurs, the size of large trucks, grazing on a

carpet of juicy ferns. The
two rows of diamond-shaped plates
went from their necks all the way
down their domed backs and almost
glowed in the sunshine.

Jamie shaded his eyes. 'They're definitely stegosaurs!'

Tom sighed. 'Too bad we haven't discovered a new dinosaur.'

'But steggies are awesome!' Jamie exclaimed as he flipped open the Fossil Finder and typed in **STEGOSAURUS**. '*THE PLATED LIZARD,*' he read. '*THE SEVENTEEN PLATES DOWN ITS BACK WERE USED FOR DISPLAY. ITS MAIN*

DEFENCE WAS THE FOUR FEARSOME
BONE SPIKES AT THE END OF ITS TAIL.'

Jamie shut his Fossil Finder and
looked at the biggest stegosaurus.
The spikes on its tail were as long as
his arm. They looked as if they were
made of steel.

'Wanna's not afraid of them,' Tom
said, as their friend trotted into the
clearing. The stegosaurs looked up as
Wanna passed, and then went back to
grazing. 'Let's follow him.'

'Keep out of the way of the steggy
spikes,' Jamie warned.

'And don't fall into a steggy cow
pat.' Tom chuckled, as they crept

up the hill towards
the herd of grazing
dinosaurs.
The steggies
were so
close
that
the

boys could hear the grinding of
dino teeth and the rumbling and
grumbling of dino digestion.

'They're so cool,' Tom whispered.

When the boys were about halfway
into the clearing, a dark shadow fell
across the hillside. Jamie looked up
to see that the sky was darkening as
thunder clouds rolled across it.

A heavy drop of rain fell on
Jamie's face, followed by another
and another. The steggies began
to shuffle away from the grass
and into the jungle at
the top of the
clearing.

'A storm's coming,' Tom said. 'We should find shelter.'

As he spoke, Wanna rushed down and nudged them under a tall broad-leafed fern in the middle of the clearing.

The sky went as dark as night and rain came pelting down. Suddenly, the hillside was lit up by a great sheet of lightning.

'The weather in the Jurassic period is wild!' Tom yelled above the noise of thunder and driving rain. Wanna shivered next to them and jumped a little as another bolt of lightning hit the ground in the clearing.

Jamie peered through the pelting rain and saw one lone stegosaurus left on the hillside. 'Why has that one stayed behind in the rain?' he asked. 'Is there something wrong with it?'

Tom wiped the lenses of his binoculars on his damp T-shirt and focused on the steggy. 'I can see a nest under its belly,' he said. 'It must be a female trying to shelter her eggs from the rain.' Tom handed the binoculars to Jamie.

Jamie zoomed in on the scooped-out nest in the ground. It contained what looked like three mud-covered

footballs. Little rivers of rainwater
were streaming down the hill,
breaking around the nest.

As Jamie watched, the rain
bucketed down even harder, making
the river turn into a torrent rushing
down the hillside. It rushed around
the mother steggy's feet. She peered
beneath her belly and brayed in
anguish.

Eee-aw, eee-aw, eee-aw!

'What's the matter?' Tom shouted. 'She sounds like a donkey with a megaphone.'

'One of her eggs is washing away,' Jamie yelled. As he watched, the egg began to tumble away from its nest and down the hill. The mother steggy brayed once more, then fell silent and stood her ground.

'She won't leave the nest with the other eggs in it,' Jamie told Tom.

'But that runaway egg might get trampled or lost in the ferns,' Tom said. 'We have to save it!'

CHAPTER 5

SEARCH:

Jamie and Tom hurtled out from
the shelter of the fern, with Wanna
grunking and following, and skidded
down the waterlogged hillside
towards the rapidly rolling egg.

Tom stuck out his foot to stop the egg. 'Gotcha!'

But the gushing water swept it over his soggy trainers.

Jamie dived head first at the egg, but the water running down the hillside changed direction and swept the slippery egg away from his outstretched hands. Jamie picked himself up, spat out a mouthful of muddy rainwater, and zig-zagged down the hillside after it. It was raining so hard he could barely see.

Suddenly Wanna appeared through the curtain of rain, trying to

catch up with the egg.
But he darted right
in front of Jamie.

Whump!

Jamie tripped
over the little
dinosaur and fell
flat on his face again. He scrambled
to his feet and zig-zagged after the
tumbling egg, bumping into Tom and
Wanna who were doing the same.
But every time the egg seemed to be
within his grasp, the water carried it
away from him.

'We've got to get below it,' Tom
shouted. 'Block it off!'

73

Jamie
and Tom hurtled
down the hill and flung
themselves sideways across
the hillside.

Thunk!

The leathery egg rolled right into
Jamie's stomach. He grabbed it and
clutched it to his chest.

'Great save!' Tom cheered as
Jamie struggled to his feet. Rain

and mud were dripping from his hair and plopping off the end of his nose. Wanna dashed up, grunking excitedly.

'Let's get out of the rain,' Jamie spluttered, tucking the heavy egg under his arm and heading for the shelter of the trees at the bottom of the hillside clearing.

They crouched beneath a canopy of ferns and examined the rain-washed egg.

'It feels like a leather football,' Tom said. 'No wonder it didn't break.'

Wanna pushed his scaly snout over Jamie's shoulder. *Slurp!* His long

reptilian tongue lapped the egg.

'You can't eat it!' Jamie told Wanna, rubbing the dinosaur dribble off the egg with a wet leaf.

In the distance, the mother steggy brayed once and fell silent.

At last, the sky began to lighten and the last raindrops plipped and plopped from the branches of the trees.

'We should put the egg back in the nest now.' Jamie carefully picked it up.

Tom, Jamie, and Wanna cautiously edged up the slippery slope towards the mother steggy. Her tail twitched as she watched them approach.

'Those spikes could spear us like sausages on a stick,' Jamie whispered nervously, as they got nearer.

'But maybe she knows we're trying to help.'

The plated lizard
was as big as a bus,
a solid domed rock
of a reptile. Jamie was
so close that he could
reach out and touch her rubbery
scales. He held out the runaway egg.
The mother steggy lowered her beaky
nose and sniffed at it suspiciously.

Her spiky tail began to swish.

Jamie, Tom, and Wanna froze. Was
she going to turn and slash at them?

The mother steggy stared first
at the egg then at Tom, Jamie, and
Wanna. At last, she blew gently
through her nostrils and stepped
back from the nest.

'She knows we've rescued her egg,'
Jamie whispered as he laid the heavy
egg back in the nest where it belonged.

As they watched, the mother steggy
bent her head over the nest and
gently licked the eggs. She watched
them closely, and the boys watched,
too. Jamie gasped as the egg that

they'd just rescued shuddered. Then
a bulge appeared on one side of the
egg.

'It's hatching!' Tom said.

The egg's leathery shell began to
rip. A tiny beaky nose pushed its way
out of the split, followed by a stumpy
little leg.

'It's bright green,' Jamie whispered.

'That will help it hide in the ferns
while it's a baby,' Tom said.

The boys and Wanna watched
as the baby stegosaurus wriggled
and squirmed to free its plump
bullfrog-sized body from the egg. At
last, it lay on top of the pieces of shell.

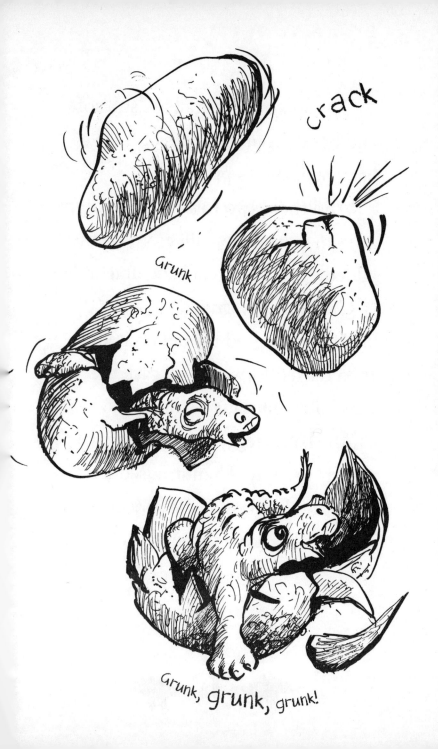

'The spikes on its tail are still soft and bent,' Tom murmured. 'Like a baby hedgehog's prickles.'

'And those two rows of tiny bumps are where its plates will grow,' Jamie added. 'It looks like a baby dragon.'

Grunk, grunk, grunk!

Wanna wagged his tail excitedly, then darted forward and gave the new baby dinosaur a slurpy lick.

The baby steggy's tail thumped weakly in reply. Then it raised its head and blinked at the sunshine that was breaking through the clouds.

CHAPTER 6

The mother stegosaurus bent over her
baby and began to lick it clean.

A chorus of rumbling noises erupted
around them. Jamie and Tom jumped
to their feet. They were surrounded
by a circle of huge stegosaurs.

'They're welcoming the new arrival,' Tom yelled above the braying. 'We'd better get out of here before they make us part of the herd.'

Jamie, Tom, and Wanna squeezed out of the tightly-packed circle, taking

care to dodge the
spikes on the end of the
gently swaying tails. Above
them, a bright rainbow was
forming in the Jurassic sky.

At the edge of the clearing, the
boys stood watching the happy scene
until their damp clothes started to
steam in the baking sunshine and the
rainbow began to fade.

'It's time we headed back to the cave,' Jamie said.

'But it's not on Gingko Hill, any more,' Tom said. 'We'll need to make a whole new map.'

'No problem!' Jamie replied. 'We'll call it Gingko Cave.'

The boys followed their trail back down the hill, through the ferns, to Gingko Cave. When they got there, Wanna paced nervously back and forth.

Tom looked worried. 'Wanna hasn't got a nest in the Jurassic. What's he going to do? Should we try to take him back with us?'

'We can't,' Jamie said. 'Everything we try to take back from Dino World turns to dust. He has to stay here.'

'But he'll be scared,' Tom said. 'He doesn't know what's out there.'

'He's a smart dinosaur. Maybe he'll adapt?' Jamie said.

Their dinosaur friend gave a little grunk. He stood back from the cave mouth, lowered his bony head, and began scratching the ground with his feet.

'He's revving up,' Jamie said.
Wanna hurtled head first towards
the rock face at the back of the cave

and, the same instant he would have hit the wall, he vanished!

'What if he's gone through to our time?' Tom wondered. 'He'll have turned to dust. We'll have lost him for ever!'

'That would be terrible.' Jamie frowned. He placed his feet nervously in the muddy version of the fossilized footprints, walking backwards, followed closely by Tom.

'One, two, three, four . . .' Jamie held his breath. 'Five!'

Jamie switched on his torch in the darkness and his heart pounded as he shone his torch on the cave floor. There was no sign of any dust.

'Wanna's safe!' Tom said, sounding relieved.

'He must have gone back home to the Cretaceous,' Jamie replied, as they squeezed back into the smugglers' cave.

'I bet he's curled up in his nest waiting for our next visit to Dino World,' Tom agreed.

The boys hurried back to the lighthouse; the museum was packed with visitors. Jamie's dad was

standing by his ammonite exhibit,
smiling broadly as a big group
of excited kids and their
parents dug fossils out
of the sand.

A young girl dusted off her fossil and walked over to the ammonite display case.

'Mine's from the Jurassic period,' she declared.

'Ah, the Jurassic,' Jamie's dad echoed wistfully. 'It was a golden age for dinosaurs and reptiles of the air and sea. It must have been a very exciting time.'

'You're right, Mr Morgan,' Tom agreed. 'The Jurassic certainly is . . . I mean was . . . a very exciting time.' He nudged Jamie and whispered, 'Hold on to that ammonite, Jamie.'

'Definitely!' Jamie grinned at Tom as he put the Jurassic ammonite safely in his backpack. Now that they knew ammonites were the keys to the past, they could go back to the Late Cretaceous or any other time period. But for now, he couldn't wait to get back to the Jurassic and meet more dinosaurs!

DINOSAUR WORLD

- - - - BOYS' ROUTE

Humungus Waterfall

Massive Canyon

Thick Jungle

Plains

Fin Rock

Jurassic Ocean

Misty
Mountains

Gingko Cave

Discovery
Hills

A Jurassic Adventure
Dinosaur Cove™
Swimming with the
Sea Monster

Special thanks to Jan Burchett and Sara Vogler
To my good friend, Roman Novotny – R.S.
To Christopher – M.S.

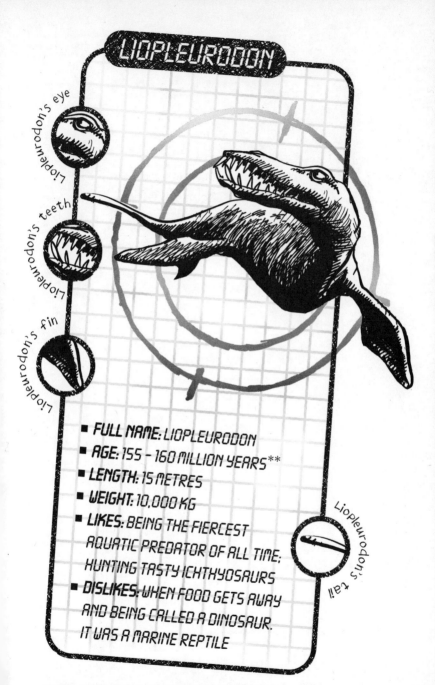

LIOPLEURODON

Liopleurodon's eye

Liopleurodon's teeth

Liopleurodon's fin

Liopleurodon's tail

- **FULL NAME:** LIOPLEURODON
- **AGE:** 155 – 160 MILLION YEARS**
- **LENGTH:** 15 METRES
- **WEIGHT:** 10,000 KG
- **LIKES:** BEING THE FIERCEST AQUATIC PREDATOR OF ALL TIME; HUNTING TASTY ICHTHYOSAURS
- **DISLIKES:** WHEN FOOD GETS AWAY AND BEING CALLED A DINOSAUR. IT WAS A MARINE REPTILE

**NOTE: SCIENTISTS CALL THIS PERIOD THE JURASSIC

Hurry up, Tom! Jamie Morgan thought as a wave lapped around his ankles, swirling the sand beneath his bare feet.

Jamie was going snorkelling in Dinosaur Cove and his best friend Tom Clay was late. He scanned

the empty beach, squinting in the sunshine.

Suddenly, he spotted Tom running across the sand with his snorkel and mask dangling over one arm, a bodyboard in the other, and his binoculars round his neck.

'You can't go bodyboarding today,' Jamie called. 'The sea's as flat as a frisbee.'

'I'm not going bodyboarding.' Tom grinned, skidding to a halt. 'In fact I'm not going in *that* sea at all.'

'Not even snorkelling?' asked

Jamie, disappointed.

Tom shook his head. 'Not here.'

'Round the headland then?' asked
Jamie. Tom had lived in Dinosaur
Cove all his life so he knew the
best places.

'No, much further away than
that.' Tom's grin was nearly splitting
his face. 'But we can be there in an
instant.'

'You mean . . .' Jamie began.

'The Jurassic ocean!' Tom finished.

Jamie and Tom shared a fantastic
secret. They'd found a way to visit a
world of living dinosaurs.

'Cool!' exclaimed Jamie. He

could already feel bubbles of
excitement inside. 'Good thing
I never go anywhere without my
backpack.'

'You've still got the Jurassic
ammonite?' Tom asked, as the boys
raced towards the cliff path on
Smuggler's Point. On their last visit,
the boys had discovered that the
ammonite fossil they carried with
them determined which time period

they visited.

'I've got it,' Jamie replied. 'But why do you have a bodyboard when we're going snorkelling?'

'It's for Wanna,' Tom explained as they neared the rocks that led up to their secret cave. 'He can ride while we swim. It's even got one of his prehistoric friends on it.' He stopped at the top of the cliff and turned the board over. A fearsome-looking

reptile with four powerful flippers had its mouth open to show off sharp, scary-looking teeth. Jamie took his Fossil Finder out of his backpack and keyed in SEA MONSTERS. 'LEE-OH-PLUR-AH-DON,' he read. 'MOST SUCCESSFUL AQUATIC HUNTER IN THE JURASSIC, THE LIOPLEURODON IS A TYPE OF PLESIOSAUR.' Jamie stuffed the Fossil Finder back into his backpack. 'Looks like a liopleurodon wouldn't

call Wanna his friend. It would call him dinner.'

The boys scrambled up the rocks to the old smugglers' cave and the hidden entrance to Dino World. They squeezed into the secret chamber at the back, and Jamie shone his torch on to the line of fossilized footprints.

'Ready for action?' said Jamie.

'You bet!' Tom replied.

They put their feet into each clover-shaped print.

'One, two, three, four . . . five!'

In an instant, Jamie and Tom were walking out among the huge trees of the Jurassic jungle. Giant dragonflies

buzzed around them like model
aeroplanes in the steaming air.

'Phew! It's as hot as ever,' said
Tom, wiping his forehead. 'Just right
for a swim.'

Grunk!

There was a rustling in the spiky
horsetail plants nearby and a little
green and brown wannanosaurus
burst out.

'Hello, Wanna!' Tom patted their dinosaur friend on his hard domed head and Wanna wagged his tail in excitement.

Jamie picked some gingkoes from an overhanging tree. 'Good job his favourite fruit grow in Cretaceous *and* Jurassic times.' He tossed two to Wanna and hid the rest in his backpack. Wanna gobbled up the smelly snacks and rushed about on his stumpy legs, giving the boys sticky licks.

Jamie took out his notebook with the new map of the Jurassic Dino World. 'This says that the sea is

south-west from the cave. Got your compass?'

'Course.' Tom pulled it out and pointed to the south-west. 'Through the trees here.'

The three friends set off over the hills, walking through the conifers and deep ferns until they arrived on the edge of a cliff, looking out over the beautiful ocean. To their right was a calm, sparkling bay shielded from the waves by a line of jet–black rocks poking up out of the water.

'Awesome!' exclaimed Tom.'With those rocks as barriers, that bay's just like a swimming pool.'

'The perfect place for snorkelling,'
said Jamie. 'And we can climb
down that pathway where the cliff's
crumbled away.'

'Last one to the beach is a sea
slug!' yelled Tom.

CHAPTER 2

'Beat you!' Jamie laughed as he clambered over the last of the slippery black slate rocks onto the sand.

'Only just,' said Tom, sliding down beside him. 'Anyway, Wanna's the sea slug.'

Wanna scampered happily
up behind.

'Do you think he remembers
our last trip to the seaside?'
asked Jamie. 'He had quite an
adventure with his flying reptile
friends.'

Tom grinned. 'Who knows what
goes on inside that domed head?'

As the boys headed along the sand,
Tom pointed to the biggest rock
out in the bay. 'That rock looks like
the back of a sea monster with a fin
sticking up in the middle.'

'We'll call it Fin Rock,' Jamie
decided. The tall rock stood like
a gate to the open sea and waves
splashed up against it on the ocean
side. Beyond the line of rocks, Jamie
could see something leaping out of
the ocean. 'Wow!'

Tom saw it too and looked
through his binoculars. 'There's more
than one!' He thrust the binoculars
at Jamie.

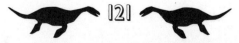

Jamie knew what they were right away. 'They're ichthyosaurs.' He flipped open his Fossil Finder and punched the keys. The image of a pointy-nosed prehistoric dolphin flashed up. *'ICK-THEE-OH-SOR,'* he read. *'ATE FISH AND SQUID. EXTINCT BY THE CRETACEOUS AGE.'*

'They look like they're having fun,' Tom said. 'We should, too. Let's go snorkelling!'

They dumped the backpack, Tom's binoculars, and their T-shirts and shoes on a dry rock, grabbed their masks and snorkels and waded into the warm shallows. Tom carried the bodyboard.

The water was so clear that Jamie could see his toes and the pebbles on the sand.

Wanna dashed after them, but skidded to a halt at the sight of the tiny waves.

'You wombat!' Tom laughed. 'They won't hurt you.'

'I know what'll get him in.' Jamie ran back onto the beach to his

backpack and pulled out a gingko
fruit.

He backed slowly into the water
keeping it just out of Wanna's reach.
The little dinosaur followed eagerly,
but when the water lapped over his
feet, he darted away again.

Jamie pretended to take a big bite
out of the stinky gingko. 'Yum, yum!'

Wanna licked his
lips then took a few
steps forwards, wading up
to his knees in the water.

'That's it, boy,'
Jamie said. 'Come
and get your tasty
snack.' He put
the gingko on the
bodyboard as Tom
held it still.

Grunk!

Wanna scrambled
on to the bodyboard
making it wobble
in the water. Jamie

held Wanna's waist as the little
dinosaur got his balance.

'He looks like a surfer now,'
chuckled Tom, letting go of the board.

'Champion of the waves,' said
Jamie.

But when Wanna bent down to
eat his gingko, he overbalanced and
somersaulted into the sea. He sat in
the shallow water
looking very
surprised.

'Poor old Wanna,' said Jamie, trying not to laugh. The boys helped him on again. This time Wanna managed to stay afloat, but looked mournfully at the gingko which was floating away. Jamie grabbed it and Wanna ate it gratefully.

'I reckon you've earned that,' said Tom.

Jamie put his hand firmly through the loop of the bodyboard's rope. 'Stay still and I'll pull you along,' he said to Wanna.

'Masks on!' declared Tom.

The boys pulled their masks over their faces.

'Check!' said Jamie.

'Snorkels in.'

Tom placed the snorkel in his mouth and gave an excited thumbs up.

The boys waded out until the water came up to their armpits and then started swimming, putting their faces in the water so that their snorkels pointed up into the air. Jamie looked down, breathing

through his snorkel. Below him, small plants waved in the gentle current and weird, colourful sea creatures darted up and down. An electric-blue sea slug crept over a rock. Then a group of squid-like creatures came swimming by. Their spiral shells were wonderful colours: blues, greens, and purples.

Real live ammonites! Jamie thought. *They're so bright.* The ammonites were nothing like the brown and grey fossils he and Tom often dug up back at Dinosaur Cove.

He could see Tom was having fun too. He made an O shape with his thumb and forefinger, the OK sign for divers. Tom signed back and made a face like a blubbery fish. Jamie burst out laughing and they both came up, gasping for air.

Wanna grunked cheerfully at them. He was obviously enjoying himself as much as they were.

The boys looked down again. A shoal of large cuttlefish drifted past. They seemed to change colour as they swam, from yellow to orange to blue. Jamie watched fascinated as their eight arms and two long tentacles explored the sand below them.

Tom dived below the water, pretending to film them as if he was making a documentary, until they disappeared into some fronds of sea kelp. But Tom wasn't paying attention to where he was swimming

and one of his legs became tangled in the underwater leaves.

As quick as he could, Jamie dived down into the tangle to pull his friend free.

'Thanks, Jamie,' Tom said as they surfaced.

'That would have made a good TV programme,' Jamie joked, adjusting his mask on his face. 'Attack of the Killer Kelp!'

Tom laughed, but stopped suddenly. 'Wait—where's the bodyboard?'

Jamie glanced down at his wrist. The rope was gone! 'It must have slipped off.' The boys looked round frantically for their little dino friend.

'Over there,' said Tom, pointing.

Wanna was sitting happily on his board, peering down into the water, completely unaware that he was drifting towards the deep, dangerous ocean beyond Fin Rock.

'Wanna!' yelled Jamie in alarm.

The boys swam quickly through the water after their friend, breathing through their snorkels so that they could swim as fast as possible. Jamie could see the seabed sloping away beneath him and the water getting deeper and deeper.

He pulled hard with his arms and kicked furiously. Glancing up through his splashes, he could see that they were nearing the wide gap in the rock barrier, and the rough, foaming water beyond. Wanna was going to be swept out to sea! Jamie couldn't let that happen.

134

Suddenly, Jamie was close enough to see the bright yellow rope ahead of him. He tried to grab it but it slipped through his fingers. Wanna and the bodyboard had reached the gap next to Fin Rock and were bobbing on the choppy water at the edge of the shallow bay. Beyond was the ocean, so deep and dark that Jamie couldn't see the bottom.

He kicked forwards again and grabbed the loop of the rope, holding on with all his strength as the board tugged against him in the rough water.

'Got him!' he yelled to Tom, his snorkel banging against his cheek.

'Just in time,' Tom said as he swam up. 'Let's get away from here.'

Jamie could feel the board wobbling violently in the waves. Wanna gave a frightened grunk.

'Don't worry, boy,' Jamie told him. 'You'll soon be safe.'

But the little dinosaur didn't seem to understand. He kicked his feet and waved his tail wildly, eyes wide with fear.

'No, Wanna!' shouted Tom. 'Stop!'

The board rocked more and more violently until . . .

SPLASH!

Wanna disappeared under the water.

CHAPTER 3

Jamie dropped the rope, took a
deep breath and dived. He caught
hold of Wanna's flailing front leg
and kicked for the surface. Wanna
emerged spluttering, then went
under again. Jamie had taken

life-guarding classes, but they hadn't gone over how to life-save a dinosaur! He swam round behind Wanna, avoiding the flapping feet, and grasped him around his neck, pulling him to the surface. Jamie had to kick hard to stay afloat as Wanna struggled in panic.

'Keep still, boy!' he spluttered, as he swam to the edge of Fin Rock. When Jamie finally reached the rock, Tom helped give Wanna a shove to get the little dinosaur up on to the flat part of Fin Rock. Jamie stayed in the water, clinging to the rock, to get his breath back.

Safely on the rock, Wanna sneezed and then spotted some seaweed.

Grunk!

He started eating the slimy leaves as if nothing had happened. Jamie smiled and hauled himself out. He pulled his mask down around his neck, like Tom had done.

'Looks like we've lost the bodyboard,' Tom said, indicating out to sea where the board floated away with the waves. 'And if scientists discover a bodyboard next to a dinosaur fossil, we could mess up all of history. Not to mention that we're going to have a hard time getting Wanna back to the beach.'

Jamie groaned. 'I'm sorry. It's all my fault.I dropped the rope.'

'You were saving me from killer kelp at the time.' Tom grinned.

 142

'Anyway, it was my stupid idea to bring Wanna snorkelling.'

Jamie watched the bodyboard being tossed about by the rough sea as he tried to think of how to get Wanna back to shore, when suddenly, a sleek, blue-grey creature jumped over the board, diving smoothly back beneath the surface.

'An ichthyosaur,' breathed Tom. 'Awesome!'

'It's two ickies,' Jamie said as another ichthyosaur batted the bodyboard with its nose, flicking it up into the air like a sea lion with a beach ball.

'Three!' yelled Tom in excitement as one more head popped up in the choppy sea. It caught the board between its teeth and swam away, its friends following behind.

'They're playing with it!' Jamie said.

'I think they're bringing it back,' said Tom.

The ichthyosaurs swam right up to Fin Rock. One of them nudged the bodyboard towards the boys.

CLICK, CLICK!

Tom and Jamie bent down to get a close look at the sleek marine reptile eyeing them from the water.

'It's smaller than the other two,' said Jamie. 'I reckon it's a young one, but it's still as big as a dolphin.'

'It has a dolphin's snout,' agreed Tom. 'Only longer and thinner. And an extra set of flippers.'

'And plenty of teeth,' Jamie replied, 'but it seems friendly. Look at that cheeky grin on its face. And those huge eyes.'

CLICK, CLICK, CLICK!

The icky gave the bodyboard
another nudge so that it banged
against the rock.

'Thanks!' Tom laughed. 'We'll be
more careful next time.' He fished
the board out of the water.

Grunk! Wanna agreed.

The icky waved its flippers and
then it chirped loudly, diving

forwards in
a perfect arc
and speeding
into the shallow
water of the bay.
Its friends
plunged after it.
'I think
they're playing
tag,' Jamie said.

Tom slid the bodyboard down
onto the calm water on the bay side
of the rock. 'Better get Wanna back
to dry land.'

Jamie put his mask on, his snorkel
back in, and then jumped into the

sea. 'Come on, boy,' he coaxed,
patting the board.

Grunk! Wanna sounded anxious.
He began to stamp his feet.

'You'll be all right, I promise,' said
Tom. 'We'll keep the board steady.'

Grunk,
   grunk,
      grunk!

Wanna was jumping
up and down now,
drumming his tail
on the rock. His
eyes were fixed on
the ocean.

'What's wrong?' asked Jamie.

'He's frightened,' said Tom.

'And so are the ickies.' In the bay
the ichthyosaurs were now circling
anxiously, making an urgent,
clamouring whistle.

Jamie pulled his mask on and ducked under the surface.

From the depths of the ocean, a huge, dark shape was swimming up through the water, heading for the bay. It had a long, crocodile-like head and four strong flippers on its massive body. It was the real-life monster on the bodyboard—a liopleurodon, the deadliest creature in the ocean.

And it was coming straight for him!

'Liopleurodon,' spluttered Jamie. 'Got to get out!'

Tom didn't waste a second. He hauled his friend on to the rock and pulled the board up after him.

'Thanks,' panted Jamie, pulling down his mask. 'That sea monster's huge.' They turned to see the lio break the surface of the water. It was at least five times as long as one of the ickies. Its massive jaws stretched like a grin, showing razor-sharp teeth that glistened in the sun.

The boys watched in horror as the lio swam straight past Fin Rock and into the bay.

'It's after the ickies,' said Tom.

The ickies waited in the bay, watching the lio approach. Suddenly, with a flick of their tails, they shot towards the gap in the rocks trying to escape into the deep ocean. But the lio was too big for the ickies to get around.

'They're trapped!' said Jamie.

The lio kept its enormous body blocking their escape route to the ocean, and each time the ickies tried to make for the open sea, the monster snapped with its fearsome teeth. The water churned like a whirlpool as the creatures struggled.

'The little one's getting tired,' said Tom.

'And that nasty lio knows it,' added Jamie grimly.

The little icky made another dash  for it, but the sea monster plunged down under the water with a

huge splash. Jamie and Tom held
their breath. When the lio's head
rose again they could see the young
ichthyosaur thrashing helplessly in its
jaws. Its friends called
to it anxiously.

'Oh no!' Jamie
felt horrible
watching the
frantic icky.

The lio
shook its prize
in triumph. But one of the ickies
dived and swam at the monster,
head-butting it hard on the soft
underside of its belly. As it turned on

its attacker, the second icky rammed
it from the other side, making the
liopleurodon let go of its prey, which
darted off to its friends.

'One-nil to the ickies!' yelled Tom,
almost falling off the rock in delight.

'They haven't won yet,' Jamie
reminded him. 'They're still trapped.'

'They helped us,' said Tom determinedly. 'We have to help them.'

'You're right,' agreed Jamie. 'But how?'

Tom quickly scanned their craggy island and went over to a spur of rock with a deep crack in it. He slid his fingers in and heaved.

'This is no time for weightlifting,' said Jamie.

'I'm not weightlifting,' puffed
Tom, red in the face with the effort.
'This rock is loose. We can . . . throw
it . . . at the lio. Might scare it off.'

Jamie helped. Soon the rock
came away. The boys picked it up
between them and staggered to the
water's edge.

'We'll give that creature
something to think
about!' shouted
Tom. 'One, *two,*
three, HEAVE!'
They lobbed the
rock as hard as they
could. It fell with

a great splash near the monster. But the lio scarcely flinched.

It ploughed on through the water after its prey. Its thick tail slapped down, splashing another huge wave over Fin Rock. The boys clung on to the fin-shaped rock, digging fingers and toes into any hold they could find. Wanna clung to the boys and grunked anxiously.

'That was close,' gasped Tom.

'Quick!' yelled Jamie. 'The bodyboard.'

The board was floating away into the bay. Tom grabbed the bodyboard's rope just in time.

'Good save,' said Jamie.

Tom was just putting the loop round his wrist to make it secure when Jamie noticed that they were in trouble. 'Uh oh!' Jamie shouted. 'The monster's seen it.'

'Wait,' Tom said. 'I've got an idea.'

Jamie saw the lio's beady eyes above the surface of the water. They were fixed on the bobbing board. 'That monster will break it to pieces,' Jamie said.

'Hang on,' Tom replied. He gave the rope a shake, making the bodyboard shudder. The liopleurodon glided towards it like a deadly crocodile after its prey, its jaws

opening wide. Suddenly it lunged,
but Tom quickly flicked the board up
and onto the rock and the lio missed
entirely.

'It's just like trout fishing,' he
shouted. 'Though I hope I don't
catch that monster!'

Jamie gave a whoop of delight.
'Go, Tom!' he called. 'The lio's

forgotten all about the ickies.'

Tom threw the board out again. Again the lio lunged and Tom jerked it away.

Jamie looked at the ickies progress and saw that they had made it to the gap in the rocks. 'The ickies are escaping!' Jamie cried, but then Tom slipped on the wet rock. He couldn't throw the board out again.

'You do it!' Tom said, throwing the rope up to Jamie.

Jamie grabbed the rope, knowing he needed to keep the monster busy until the ichthyosaurs were safely away. He flung the bodyboard out

like Tom had done—
but this time the
liopleurodon was
ready. As soon as
it saw the bright

splash!

board slapping down onto the water
it grabbed it in its teeth and pulled
hard. Jamie didn't have a chance to
let go of the rope.

He was catapulted off the rock and
into the water!

The water roared in Jamie's ears as he
was dragged along the surface by the
sea monster into the bay. White foam
swirled around him, and he wished
he had had his mask on. Everything

was blurry, but he could still see through the water. Suddenly the pulling stopped. Jamie looked ahead and could just make out through the water that the liopleurodon had turned. It floated on the water, its beady eyes just above the surface. They were looking straight at him.

It let go of the bodyboard.

Oh no, thought Jamie. *I'm dinner!*

As the huge grey body slipped under the surface of the water, coming towards him, Jamie swam frantically for the rock.

He could just hear Tom shouting, 'Hurry, Jamie!'

Jamie knew he
couldn't out-swim the lio, but
then he remembered something
Tom had told him about predators
losing interest when their prey
stopped moving. He had nothing to
lose. Jamie took a huge breath and
stopped swimming.

He quickly made a star with his arms and legs and lay there, floating face down in the water.

He watched, his heart pounding hard, as the lio swam in a circle below, watching him.

Jamie knew he mustn't move a muscle. The bodyboard rope was still tied round his wrist, tugging at him. He had to fight to keep his arm still, but his plan was working! The sea monster wasn't attacking any more. It had lost interest. But Jamie knew that as soon as he lifted his head for air it could be back on to him like a shot.

Please go! he thought, desperately willing the sea monster to swim away. But it didn't. Jamie felt as if his lungs were going to burst.

Suddenly he heard a great barrage of squeaking, clicking, and whistling in the water. Something was coming

173

from the deep ocean. The lio had heard it too. It whipped round to see what it was. Jamie took his chance. He lifted his head and gulped in air.

Then he saw a wonderful sight. A large pod of sleek grey ichthyosaurs was speeding towards the bay. They

leapt over the waves, calling to each other—and Jamie could see their three little icky friends leading the charge!

They made straight for the lio and began to ram it from all sides. It thrashed about trying to ward off the furious attack.

Jamie struck out for the rock and, with Tom's help, scrambled out of the water. Wanna grabbed the bodyboard in his teeth and pulled it on to the rock.

'Go, ickies!' yelled Tom. 'You can beat that monster.'

The lio reared and plunged, thrashing out angrily to shake off the whirling mass of ickies. But there were too many for it. They battered and rammed from all sides.

The boys and Wanna watched as the beast swished its massive tail, sending a final huge wave breaking over Fin Rock, then fled for the open sea.

Jamie and Tom leapt up and down in delight while Wanna grunked eagerly. The sea monster had been beaten!

'That was awesome!' breathed Jamie.

'Those ickies saved your life.' Tom grinned.

Jamie nodded. 'Too right! They fought off the fiercest creature in the Jurassic ocean!'

'And they look really pleased about it,' said Tom, pointing.

The pod of ickies was swimming all around Fin Rock, their sleek bodies arcing in and out of the waves. Wanna grunked happily at them.

'Thank you!' Jamie shouted. 'You were great.' He turned to Tom. 'Shame we don't know icky language.'

'Looks like they understood anyway,' replied Tom. The ickies were sending back a chorus of clicks and whistles. 'I think they're saying, "You're welcome".'

'Let's get back to dry land,' said Jamie, putting his mask back on.

 182

'Hop on board, Wanna. The water's safe now.'

Grunk! Wanna looked at the bodyboard which was punctured with large liopleurodon teeth holes.

'Don't worry, boy,' Tom assured him. 'It's still seaworthy.'

Jamie slid into the water, pulling the bodyboard behind him. Tom held it steady and Wanna wobbled on board. Holding one side each, the boys kicked off for shore.

'I can hear something behind us,' Tom shouted suddenly.

Jamie spun round, spluttering as his mouth filled with water. Then he burst out laughing. 'We've got an escort.'

It was the three young ickies swimming along behind the boys, clicking and whistling.

Soon Jamie and Tom were close enough to the shore to stand in the waist-deep water.

The smallest icky swam round their legs, gently butting them as if to say goodbye. Then it sped off to its friends and the three of them

swam swiftly away, heading for the
open sea.

'Thanks again,' called Jamie after
them, pulling off his mask entirely.

Grunk!

Wanna jumped off the bodyboard
and splashed the last few steps to
the beach.

The boys picked up their
things and made their way back
to the cave. Jamie pointed to
the huge teeth marks in Tom's
board. 'How are we going to
explain this?'

'We could say it got attacked by
a shark?' suggested Tom.

'No one will believe that,' Jamie replied.

'Well, they won't believe what really happened to it.'

Wanna stuck out his tongue and gave the bodyboard a lick. Then he trotted off towards the cave. When they got close, Wanna began to gather leaves and twigs in his teeth.

'He's making himself a nest,' said Tom.

'Let's help,' said Jamie, grabbing a handful of ferns. The boys got to work, gathering sticks and ferns.

Wanna laid a few twigs down, then nudged them here and there, but

when Jamie
went to put
some branches
into the structure
Wanna grunked loudly.

'I think he's saying they're
the wrong way round.' Tom laughed.

Jamie flipped the branches over.
'Is that better?'

Grunk, grunk!

Wanna wagged his tail. Soon he
was curled up in his Jurassic nest.

'Sleep tight, boy,' said Tom. The
boys had seen on their last visit that
Wanna knew how to go back to the
Cretaceous any time he wanted, so

they said goodbye to their faithful
friend and stepped backwards in
the footprints.

As the boys emerged into the bright
sunlight of Dinosaur Cove they were
surprised to see a crowd of people
gathered on the shoreline below.

'What's going on?' Tom asked.

'There's Grandad,' said Jamie. 'Let's
find out.'

They scrambled down to the beach
as fast as they could.

Everyone was staring and pointing
out to sea. Tom made sure he kept
the bodyboard behind him so no one
would notice the teeth marks.

'I was wondering where you two
had got to,' Grandad called when he
spotted them. 'You've been missing
all the fun.'

He nodded out towards the bay.
As the boys watched, the enormous
body of a sleek grey creature broke
the surface of the sea. A tall spout of
water shot into the air. A moment

later, a gigantic whale leapt out of the waves. The crowd clapped and cheered.

'Don't see many whales in these parts.' Grandad beamed.

'Looks like Dinosaur Cove has got its own sea monster,' Jamie whispered to Tom with a wink.

'But not as scary as the one back in Dino World,' Tom whispered back.

'I definitely prefer this one,' Jamie said.

DINOSAUR WORLD

- - - - BOYS' ROUTE

Massive Canyon

Humungus Waterfall

Thick Jungle

Plains

Fin Rock

Jurassic Ocean

192

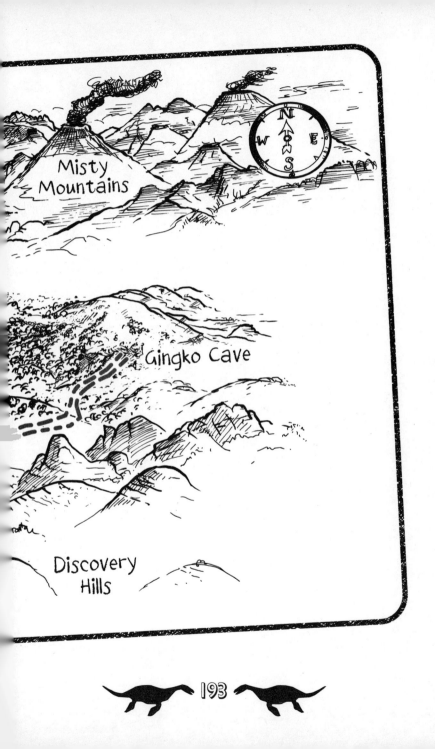

Misty
Mountains

Gingko Cave

Discovery
Hills

A Jurassic Adventure

Dinosaur Cove™

Tracking the
Gigantic Beast

Special thanks to Jane Clarke

For Andy and Rob, with love - R.S.

For my Hannah, at last - M.S.

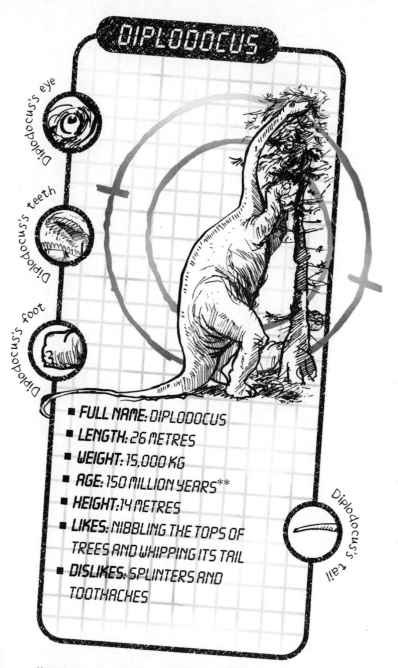

DIPLODOCUS

Diplodocus's eye

Diplodocus's teeth

Diplodocus's foot

Diplodocus's tail

- **FULL NAME:** DIPLODOCUS
- **LENGTH:** 26 METRES
- **WEIGHT:** 15,000 KG
- **AGE:** 150 MILLION YEARS**
- **HEIGHT:** 14 METRES
- **LIKES:** NIBBLING THE TOPS OF TREES AND WHIPPING ITS TAIL
- **DISLIKES:** SPLINTERS AND TOOTHACHES

NOTE: SCIENTISTS CALL THIS PERIOD THE JURASSIC

'Where are you, Grandad?' Jamie Morgan's voice echoed round the dinosaur museum on the ground floor of the lighthouse. 'We're off to hunt for dinosaurs!'

'He'll think we mean fossil dinosaurs, not real ones,' Tom Clay whispered. The two friends grinned at one another. Only they knew the amazing secret of Dinosaur Cove— a cave that led to a world of real live dinosaurs! 'Grandad?' Jamie called again. As he slung his backpack over his shoulders and stepped into the lobby of the museum, his feet scrunched on something gritty.

'Why are these seeds all over the floor?' Tom wondered. 'Maybe he's gardening?'

They hurried out of the front door and looked around the cliff top. There was no sign of Grandad.

There was a flash of yellow as a little bird with a red head swooped down and began to peck at something on a flat rock beside a bush near the edge of the cliff.

'Look,' Tom said, pointing to the trail of seeds that led to the rock where the bird was feasting. The branches of the bush rustled.

'Grandad?' Jamie called, making the bird fly off.

'Shhhhh!' hissed the bush.

Jamie laughed in surprise as Grandad's mop of unruly hair emerged from the leaves.

'What are you doing in a bush?' Jamie asked, running over.

'This is my bird hide,' Grandad whispered. 'I'm taking part in a survey, recording all the different birds that visit Dinosaur Cove. That was a goldfinch.'

'Sorry, we scared it away,' Tom said.

'It'll come back to the birdseed.'
The captain's eyes twinkled. 'It can't
resist the bait. Why don't you boys
try a spot of bird watching?' shhhhh!

'Awesome idea! We know
just the place to do it.' Jamie
nudged Tom.

Grandad held
up his finger.

'Remember, the secret of bird watching is stay quiet and hidden.' He tapped his nose, then ducked back into the bush.

'See you later, Grandad!' Jamie called.

They raced off along the path towards Smuggler's Point.

'Got the ammonite?' Tom asked.

Jamie patted his pocket. 'The Jurassic one,' he confirmed as they reached the cave. The spiral fossil was the key to which time period they would visit.

Jamie took out his torch and they squeezed through the tiny gap at

the back of the cave into the secret chamber that led to Dino World. His heart was thumping with excitement as he fitted his feet into the fossil footprints. He took a deep breath and stepped towards the cave wall. 'One, two, three, four . . . FIVE!'

A crack of light appeared in the solid rock and suddenly he was in the sweltering sunlight of Dino World.

His ears filled with the sounds of insects buzzing and the strange calls of unseen creatures out there in the Jurassic jungle.

There was a squelch as Tom trod on the slimy leaf mould beside him, stirring up a familiar smell in the hot humid air.

'Phew!' Tom gagged. 'The gingko fruit must be ripe. They're even stinkier than usual.'

'Wanna will love them.' Jamie pulled a face.

At the mention of his name, a little dinosaur with a bony head bounded up to the boys on his

two back legs, wagging his tail and making happy grunking noises.

'He's pleased to see us.' Tom laughed. 'It's good to see you again, Wanna.'

Wanna looked up hopefully at the fruit-laden gingko tree.

'I'll get you one.' Jamie wrinkled his nose and reached out for an apricot-sized fruit on a nearby branch. It was so ripe that sticky gingko goo squished through his fingers. He tried to toss the fruit to the little dinosaur but it stuck fast to his hand.

'Yuck!' Jamie held out his hand. Wanna slurped down the fruit, then

licked the sticky juice off Jamie's
fingers with his sandpaper tongue.

'Gross!' Jamie wiped off the dino
drool on to his jeans.

'Since Wanna's so mad
about gingkoes,' Tom said
thoughtfully,

'maybe we should take some along to bait flying reptiles, like birdseed.'

'We'll be the very first Jurassic birdwatchers.'

Jamie filled a plastic bag with the foul-smelling fruit and stuffed it in his backpack. He held out his hands for Wanna to clean.

'Let's go dino bird watching!'

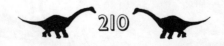

CHAPTER 2

SEARCH:

G H I J K L M N
... Y Z [END]

Tom and Jamie plunged into the
steamy Jurassic jungle, and began
to wade through the sea of ferns
beneath the tall conifer trees. Wanna
followed them closely, with his eyes
firmly fixed on Jamie's backpack.

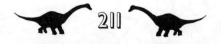

Tom looked up.

'What is it?' Jamie asked, pushing a fern out of his face.

'I can't see anything,' Tom complained as another fern twanged to and fro in front of his face. 'We need to find a gap in the jungle.'

They pressed on through the thick undergrowth until they came to a clearing scattered with enormous flat rocks.

'This looks like a good place for bird watching,' Tom said. 'Where shall we hide?'

Jamie looked round. 'How about up there?' He pointed to a tall tree on the edge of the clearing. It was draped with thick rope-like vines. Halfway up, two sturdy branches emerged from the trunk together, making a safe platform to sit on.

'Looks good,' Tom agreed, 'but the birds might see us.'

'Not if we make a dino-bird hide!' Jamie said excitedly.

'Cool,' Tom grinned. 'Like a tree house.'

'We can use ferns for the roof and sides . . . ' Jamie grabbed hold of the thick stem of a broad leaf fern and pulled with all his might. 'I can't pull it up,' he panted, 'it's too tough.'

As he spoke, the fern gave way with a sudden pop and he fell backwards into the soggy leaf mould. He stood up covered in mud, with pine needles and bits of dead fern sticking all over him.

'I look like a swamp monster,' he spluttered.

Tom laughed. 'But it's awesome camouflage. A bit more and you'll look like part of the jungle.' He grabbed a handful of tender fern tips and stuffed them down the neck of Jamie's T-shirt.

'I'll get you for that!' Jamie scooped up an armful of soft mud and leaf mould and hurled it towards Tom.

Tom stepped sideways and the muck hit Wanna. *Splat!*

Splat!

'Missed me!' Tom burst into laughter at the sight of the muck-covered dinosaur. Wanna didn't seem to like that. He wagged his tail and lowered his head.

'Go, Wanna, go!' Jamie cheered as Wanna gently barged Tom into the muddy ooze. Jamie rushed over and stuffed some fern tips down his friend's neck.

'Now you're camouflaged too!' Jamie bent double laughing.

After a moment, Tom struggled to his feet. 'We'll scare away the wildlife with all this noise. Let's get on with making the hide.'

The boys both gathered an armful of dead leaves, then climbed the tree and began weaving them through the dangling vines to make the sides of the hide.

Down below, Wanna put his head on one side and watched curiously. Then he sighed deeply and curled up in the ferns.

'Wanna's taking a nap,' Jamie whispered, peering down at the little dinosaur through a gap in the fern wall.

'That's good,' Tom said, laying the last of the ferns across the top of the hide to make a roof. 'Let's hope he stays still and quiet.'

Jamie took out his notebook and wrote DINO BIRD SURVEY at the top of one page. Tom smiled, then they peered out through the fern wall into the clearing, watching and waiting.

After a few minutes, something flapped onto the branch of the tree above them.

Through a gap in the fern roof, Jamie could see the claws on the creature's feet gripping on to the

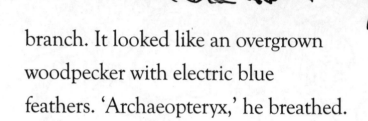

branch. It looked like an overgrown
woodpecker with electric blue
feathers. 'Archaeopteryx,' he breathed.

'Awesome,' Tom whispered. 'Its
beak's full of razor-sharp teeth.'

As Jamie leaned closer, the fern tips
sticking out of his T-shirt tickled his
nose. 'A . . . a . . . atishoo!' he sneezed.

The archaeopteryx took off in an
explosion of twigs. Something white

and slimy splattered on the fern
roof of the hide and dripped down,
narrowly missing Jamie's shoulder.

'Yurgh!' Tom grimaced.
'. . . Archaeopteryx poo!'
Jamie smiled and opened his
notebook to the dino bird survey
page. He wrote 'Archaeopteryx 1'
and sketched a picture of the bird.

220

They had seen an archaeopteryx on an earlier adventure in Dino World. Jamie hoped the next entry would be something new and even more exciting.

'Let's put out some gingkoes,' Tom whispered, taking the plastic bag out of Jamie's backpack.

'Don't wake Wanna,' Jamie warned him. 'Or he'll eat them all.'

As quietly as he could, Tom stretched up his arm and squished a

gingko fruit onto a branch, sticking it down.

'Let's see what takes the bait,' he whispered.

The boys sat peering through the gaps in the ferns, waiting for the dino birds.

Nothing came. Jamie shifted uncomfortably on the branch. It was hard sitting still and waiting, but the boys were determined. Tom flipped open the Fossil Finder to pass the time. He tapped in

in *JURASSIC FLYING REPTILES*. 'My favourite flier's the dimorphodon,' he told Jamie. 'It has a beak like a puffin.'

'Shh,' Jamie whispered.

Just then, the branches of the conifer rustled as a dark orange pterosaur with a wingspan as wide as Jamie's outstretched arms landed on the branch.

'Is it a dimorphodon?' Tom asked.

The creature scooped up a jawful of gingko fruit, dangling its long thin tail with a kite-shaped tip in front of their noses.

223

'No, that's a rhamphorhynchus,' Jamie whispered excitedly, noting it down on his dino bird survey.

Tom looked closely at the flying reptile's long, thin jaws. 'Its teeth criss-cross,' he said in surprise.

Jamie started to sketch the creature.

Thunk!

Thunk!

The tree
trunk wobbled
and Jamie only
just managed
to hang on to
his notebook.
Beneath them,
Wanna was standing
back from the tree. He lowered
his head and barged it into the trunk.

Thunk! The tree wobbled again.
The rhamphorhynchus launched
itself into the air with a squawk.

'Stop it, Wanna!' Tom called
down. 'You'll scare everything away.'

'He must be bored,' Jamie said. 'A

Thunk!

few gingkoes will keep him quiet.'
He dropped a stinky fruit, which
splattered at Wanna's feet. But the
little dinosaur took no notice.
He head-butted the tree again.

Tom and Jamie looked at each
other.

'I don't believe it,' Jamie gasped.

'Wanna never ignores gingkoes.'

'Something's wrong,' Tom said nervously.

The tree shook.

'That wasn't Wanna,' Tom gulped. 'Wanna's trying to warn us. Something's coming!'

CHAPTER 3

A humongous dappled-green lizardy head burst through the front wall of their fern hide, tearing it clean away.

'Get down!' Jamie shouted as the creature swept off the flimsy roof and opened its toothy jaws.

The boys flattened themselves against the thick branch they were sitting on.

Scruuuuunch!

The tree shook as the long-necked dinosaur stripped the vines from the branch above them.

Tom gulped. 'What is it?'

The gigantic beast grabbed hold of another branch and raked off the

pine needles, chewing the greenery with its peg-like teeth.

Jamie heaved a huge sigh of relief. 'It's a plant eater.'

Tom grinned. 'And with those nostrils on the top of its snout, it's got to be a diplodocus!' Jamie pulled out his Fossil Finder and looked up diplodocus. 'IT EATS TONS OF VEGETATION A DAY TO FUEL ITS HUGE BODY, BUT DOESN'T STOP TO CHEW,' he read. 'IT SWALLOWS STONES TO GRIND UP ITS FOOD.'

'Cool,' Tom said. 'It's an eating machine.'

Jamie stashed the Fossil Finder and his notebook in his backpack as the diplodocus's nose swept away the rest of the fern hide. It sniffed deeply and moved towards Jamie. Its long neck and head were covered in giraffe-like markings in shades of jungle green.

'Keep still,' Tom hissed. 'It wants to eat your ferns, not you!'

The dinosaur's rubbery lips nuzzled at the fresh fern tips sticking out of the neck of Jamie's T-shirt.

'It tickles!' Jamie giggled as the lizardy lips nibbled at the leaves.

Below them, Wanna had settled down, realizing that they weren't in danger.

Tom pulled the fern leaves out of his shirt and held them out on the palm of his hand. 'Here you are.'

The gigantic beast took them gently and gulped them down.

'It's like feeding a huge horse,' Tom whispered.

The boys watched as the diplodocus stripped more branches of pine needles and swallowed some of the smaller twigs whole, leaving bare branches draped with dinosaur drool.

'This tree would make better dino toothpicks than lunch,' Jamie commented.

'There are some younger creepers and branches at the top, Dippy,' Tom said. 'Those would be tastier.'

As if it'd heard, the huge dino reared up on its hind legs.

'Awesome!' Jamie murmured. They could see the diplodocus's pale yellow

tummy as its elephantine front legs
pawed the air and it stretched out its
long neck to grab the thickest branch
at the top of the tree.

The branch bent, but instead of
raking off the leaves and the
creepers, the dinosaur hung
on to it. The whole tree
began to bend and shake.

'Dippy! Let go of the
branch,' Tom shouted,
hugging the
shuddering tree.

There was a
craaack as the
branch broke off

and a thump as the
diplodocus's feet hit
the earth. The tree
swayed back and forth,
but the boys managed
to cling to their branch.
'Phew!' Jamie
breathed.

Beneath them,
they could see Dippy
contentedly champing at
the branch, breaking it
into small pieces to gulp
down. Suddenly, the

dinosaur's eyes bulged and it swung
its head up and began to shake it
violently from side to side, making
frantic sucking sounds with
its tongue.

'What's happening now?' Tom
looked worried.

'I'm not sure,' Jamie replied, 'but
it doesn't look good.'

The dinosaur's movements
became even more erratic and the

boys worried about Wanna getting
trampled on the ground.

'Dippy's freaking out!' Tom
yelled. 'Let's get out of here before it
knocks us off.'

But before they could scramble
down the tree, Dippy started to

bellow, rearing up on its hind legs
and thrashing its front feet.

'Hang on,' Jamie yelled as two
huge dinosaur feet flailed at the tree.

The tree bent and sprang back,
catapulting Tom off the branch.
Jamie watched helplessly as his friend

fell, clawing wildly at the air. Luckily, he landed on the diplodocus's neck, wrapping his arms around it to stop himself falling further.

'I meant hang on to the tree, not the dinosaur!' Jamie yelled as the huge dinosaur stomped into the jungle with Tom swinging from its long, swaying neck.

CHAPTER 4

From his tree, Jamie could see Dippy
shaking its head wildly from side to
side. Any minute now, Tom would
fall off or be crushed against a tree
trunk. He had to save his friend!

The end
of a thick creeper
dangled before
him. Jamie took a
deep breath, grabbed
on to the vine and
launched himself
towards the next
tree. He swung safely
across to a thick branch
with more vines

Help!

hanging down.
He took hold and
leapt off, swinging
from tree to tree
through the jungle
after Tom.

Beneath him,
Wanna was

leaping logs and dodging branches in his struggle to keep up.

'Yee-haw!' Jamie called as he swung, and soon he was alongside the lumbering diplodocus.

Tom had slipped round the underside of the dinosaur's neck, just below its head, and was clinging on for dear life.

'Help!' Tom shouted at the top of his lungs. 'I can't hold on much longer!'

'I'll get you,' Jamie shouted back. He launched himself onto another vine and swung across Dippy's path. 'Grab my hand!'

The boys'
fingertips brushed
as Jamie swung past the dinosaur's
eyes, but he wasn't close enough to
reach Tom.

Dippy stopped thrashing its head
and looked in amazement as Jamie
swung back on to the tree.

'I'm coming again.' Jamie took a deep breath and launched himself from the same vine. He swung towards Tom, rising higher and higher, right above the dino's head! At the top of the swing, he stretched his hand down to Tom. Tom reached up, and they interlocked their fingers.

Jamie had him!

Snap! The vine gave way.

Jamie plummeted down, and was only saved by his friend's firm grip. While Tom held on to Dippy's neck with all his might, Jamie pulled himself up towards the giant reptile's scaly head and clawed for a handhold.

248

He grabbed what felt like a slimy
rubbery ledge. He was dangling from
Dippy's spitty bottom lip.

Whooooooooo!

Dippy dropped its head and
Jamie quickly let go and tumbled to
the ground. Tom landed in a heap
beside him.

As Dippy pulled away, Jamie
could see a piece of wood the size of
a baseball bat lodged between the
dinosaur's brown teeth and rubbery
green gums.

'That was awesome!' Tom gasped.
'I've never swung from a dinosaur
before.'

'First time for me, too,' Jamie panted, trying to catch his breath as he untangled himself from his backpack.

Wanna hurtled out of the jungle and leapt on them, grunking enthusiastically.

'Gerroff, we're ok!' Jamie struggled to his feet.

grunk!

grunk

grunk

Whoooooo!

Dippy was wailing again, scraping its jaws along the ground. Then it lifted its head and shook it from side to side.

'I know what's making it so crazy,' Jamie told Tom. 'I saw a splinter of branch stuck between its teeth.'

As they watched the huge dinosaur stomp off again, Tom said, 'Poor Dippy's got a toothache.'

Jamie nodded. 'I had toothache once and it really hurt.'

'We need a dinosaur dentist,' Tom said, 'but we can't just call one up.'

The boys looked at each other and grinned.

'Let's go after it,' Jamie said.

Tom nodded. 'We'll be Dippy's dentists!'

CHAPTER 5

'Follow Dippy!' Tom set
off in the direction of a series of
circular dents in the leaf mould on
the jungle floor.

Wanna dashed ahead and
stopped at a mound of slimy

orange mush, bobbing his head up and down.

'Good thing Dippy's left a clear trail,' Jamie commented.

'He's squashed ferns too,' Tom pointed out a heap of crushed fronds.

Something wet and slimy splattered down Jamie's neck. Slimy strings of frothy saliva were dripping from the tree Dippy had been walking under.

'Dino drool,' he told Tom. 'Dippy must have scraped its mouth against the branch to try and get that splinter out of its jaw.'

The trail led them to a part of the jungle criss-crossed with pathways and dinosaur footprints.

'Other diplodocus are using these paths,' Jamie said in dismay. 'I can't make out Dippy's trail.'

The boys scanned the jungle.

'I think it went this way.' Tom set off along a well-trodden jungle path, but Wanna grabbed his sleeve and dug his heels into the ground.

Jamie laughed. 'I think Wanna thinks you're going the wrong way.'

Wanna let go of Tom and then set off at a brisk trot down another pathway.

The boys chased after Wanna and soon burst into a clearing scattered with enormous flat rocks.

'We're back where we started!' Jamie exclaimed. 'We've gone round in a circle.'

'There's Dippy.' Tom pointed to the far side of the rocks. 'It looks exhausted.'

The huge dinosaur was dragging its enormous feet and staggering. As they

watched, Dippy's
legs buckled and it fell with a
humongous

CRASH!

The earth shuddered beneath
Tom's and Jamie's feet and there
was a moment's silence in the jungle

before the insects resumed their relentless buzzing.

Dippy lay on its side, with its long neck and tail stretched out.

'Oh no,' Jamie said. 'Is it dead?'

'No,' Tom replied. 'Its rib cage is moving and there's froth bubbling from its mouth. It's just exhausted. We can still help.'

They hurried towards the collapsed dinosaur. Its beady eyes looked at them, but it didn't move.

Oily tears oozed from Dippy's eyes. It opened its mouth with a pitiful low. *Whoooooooooo.*

'We've got to get that splinter out,' Tom said. 'If it's too exhausted to move, the Jurassic scavengers will get it.'

'A real dentist would get it out in no time,' Jamie said.

'It'd never fit in a dentist's chair!' Tom joked.

Jamie and Tom lay on their tummies and wriggled up to the dinosaur's mouth. A blast of warm dino breath and frothy saliva hit them full in the face.

'Yuck!' Jamie gagged. 'Its breath smells like rotten eggs.'

'I can't see the splinter,' Tom said, wiping the froth away from Dippy's

jaws. 'We need to get rid of some of
this spit.'

Jamie helped and soon the boys
could see Dippy's teeth, like two
rows of brown tent pegs set in
rubbery green gums. The splinter
was stuck in its gum between two
back teeth.

'I think I can get it out.' Jamie
gently reached his arm inside the

261

dinosaur's mouth and
grabbed the end of
the splinter. The
dippy's mouth felt
warm and slimy.
Whooooooooo.
The gigantic beast
moaned but kept still.

'Careful,' Tom breathed.

'Open wide, Dippy.' Jamie tugged
at the splinter, but his hands only
slipped down the wood.

'Do real dentists get covered in this
much spit?' Jamie groaned. 'I can't
get a good grip.'

'Let me try,' Tom told him.

Jamie wriggled to one side and wiped the dino drool on his jeans while Tom reached in.

'It's much too slimy,' Tom agreed.

Dippy closed his eyes as the boys sat back on their heels.

'We're not helping; we're just hurting it more,' Tom said with a frown.

Above them came the sound of flapping wings. Dark grey shapes began to circle like vultures above the exhausted diplodocus.

'Pterodactyls.' Jamie leapt to his feet and shook his fists at them. 'Go away!' he yelled.

Wanna took one
look at them and
dashed into the jungle.

The sharp-beaked
pterodactyls flapped
onto the branch of a nearby
tree and sat there, hunched
and waiting.

CHAPTER 6

Wanna crept back into the clearing with a mouthful of soft juicy ferns, and put them straight into Dippy's mouth.

Dippy half-heartedly spat them out.

'It's a good idea to feed it.' Tom patted Wanna's head. 'But it's in too much pain to eat.'

'It'll die if we give up on it,' Jamie said, glancing up at the pterodactyls. 'We have to keep trying. How can we get a better grip on that splinter?'

Wanna began hopping from foot to foot, grunking hopefully.

'He wants a gingko,' Tom said. 'You'd better give him one or he'll never let us get on with it.'

Jamie got out the plastic bag. All the remaining gingko fruit were squashed together in a stinky sticky mess.

'Yuck!' He opened the bag and lay it on the ground in front of Wanna. Wanna sniffed at the bag but didn't make a move to eat the gingkoes; he just looked at Jamie, panting.

Jamie tried to wipe off the foul smelling juice on his T-shirt, but it was stuck fast to his hands.

'That's what Wanna was trying to tell us,' Jamie said. 'We can

use gingko glue!' He took another handful of mushy gingkoes out of the bag and wriggled on his tummy up to Dippy's jaws.

Tom grabbed a handful of gingko pulp as well and crawled over to help.

Jamie gently mashed the gooey gingkoes along the splinter of wood. 'It's sticking!'

Tom knelt beside Jamie. 'I'll grab on too.'

Together they started pulling. 'It's moving,' Jamie said. There was a sucking, squelching sound then the boys fell backwards as the splinter came free.

Whooo!

Dippy seemed relieved.

The splinter was as long as Jamie's arm with a sharp point, covered

271

in mucus. Jamie tossed it into the undergrowth and then watched as Wanna nudged the soft ferns towards the huge dinosaur. Dippy gulped them down and raised its head.

Sluuurp! Sluurp! Sluurp!

A wet tongue the size of a bath towel, covered in spitty bits of fern and gingko goo, licked each of them in turn.

'He's going to be OK.' Jamie and

Sluuurp!

Sluuurp!
Sluurp!

Tom leaped to their feet and shouted out in celebration. The vulture-like pterodactyls in the tree took off in alarm.

Dippy slowly clambered to its feet. Then it gently lowered its head and nuzzled first the boys, then Wanna, before turning and lumbering off into the forest.

'We did it!' Jamie grinned, wiping diplodocus drool off his face with the back of his hand. 'We are dino dentists!'

They gave each other a high five. Gingko goop spattered down their bare arms.

'Help, Wanna!' Jamie and Tom shouted together, holding out their arms. They cringed as Wanna's sandpapery tongue rasped off every trace of gingko juice.

'It's probably time to go,' Jamie said.

'But we haven't seen a dimorphodon,' Tom said.

'We've used all the gingkoes,'
Jamie reminded him, 'so we can't
bait any more birds.'

'I suppose we've done enough
"bird" watching for one day,'
Tom agreed as they set off for
Gingko Cave. 'Archaeopteryx,
rhamphorhynchus, and those
horrible pterodactyls.'

As they came to the clearing in
front of the shallow cave, Jamie put
his arm out to stop Tom. He put his
finger to his lips.

'Look,' he whispered. The ground
was splattered with slimy ripe
gingkoes. Waddling among them was

a sand-coloured creature, the size of
a cat, with leathery wings and a long
spiky tail.

The boys watched as it sank its big red beak into the stinky fruit.

'Dimorphodon.' Tom whispered. 'My favourite flier.'

The boys watched it for a moment until Wanna hurtled out of the jungle and the dimorphodon took off, flapping away over the tree tops, honking as it flew. Wanna skidded to a halt and started to slurp up the gingkoes.

Jamie smiled. 'Wanna is rubbish at bird watching.'

'He likes the bait too much,' Tom replied. 'See you next time, Wanna!'

The little dinosaur lifted his snout from the gingkoes and wagged his tail as the boys stepped backwards into the footprints. The ground turned to stone beneath their feet and once more they were back in the

secret chamber at the
back of the smugglers'
cave.

'Dino dentistry has made me hungry,' Jamie said, as they dashed to the lighthouse.

'Grandad!' he called from the lighthouse door. 'We're back! We're so hungry we could eat a dinosaur.'

'Up here, me hearties,' came the answering cry. The boys raced up the stairs to the kitchen.

'I'll make some of my famous cheese and pickle sandwiches,' the captain told them with a grin.

OWWWWW!

'They'll only take a couple of minutes.'

'I can't wait that long.' Jamie spotted his grandad's jar of boiled sweets. He grabbed one and bit into it.

'Owwwww! My tooth!' he yelled.

'You're making more noise than a dinosaur at the dentist,' Tom told him.

Jamie spluttered. 'Not as much noise as someone swinging from the neck of a diplodocus.'

'I wish I had your imaginations.' Grandad laughed as he cut up the sandwiches. 'You sound as if you've had a fun day.'

Jamie and Tom grinned at each other.

'We always have fun in Dinosaur Cove!'

DINOSAUR WORLD

- - - - BOYS' ROUTE

Humongous
Waterfall

Massive Canyon

Plains

Fin Rock

Jurassic
Ocean

Misty
Mountains

Thick
Jungle

Gingko
Cave

scovery
Hills

GLOSSARY

Ammonite (am-on-ite) – an extinct animal with octopus-like legs and often a spiral-shaped shell that lived in the ocean.

Archaeopteryx (ar-kee-op-ter-ix) – the earliest bird capable of flight, with sharp teeth, three clawed fingers, and a long bony tail. Archaeopteryx was not a fussy feeder, eating small animals, plants, and insects.

Dimorphodon (di-mor-foh-don) – a flying reptile that had a long, pointed tail and big head with two different types of teeth.

Diplodocus (dip-lod-oh-kus) – one of the longest land dinosaurs with a long neck and whip-like tail. This huge dinosaur had pencil-shaped blunt teeth perfect for its plant-only diet.

Gingko (gink-oh) – a tree native to China called a 'living fossil' because fossils of it have been found dating back millions of years, yet they are still around today. Also known as the stink bomb tree because of its smelly apricot-like fruit.